By Wiley Blevins

Illustrated by Elliot Kreloff

RED
CHAIR
•PRESS•™

Rocking Chair Kids books are published by Red Chair Press.

Red Chair Press LLC   PO Box 333   South Egremont, MA 01258

www.redchairpress.com

Publisher's Cataloging-In-Publication Data

Blevins, Wiley.
  Count on it / by Wiley Blevins ; illustrated by Elliot Kreloff. -- [First edition].

    pages : illustrations ; cm. -- (Rocking chair kids. Basic concepts)

  Summary: Gigi is planning a Gigi and the Three Bears theme party. With nine friends coming, readers help Gigi count what she needs from 0 to 10. This book introduces young children to the basic concept of counting from 0 to 10.

  Edition statement supplied by publisher.

  Interest age level: 000-005.

  Issued also as an ebook (978-1-63440-086-2).

  ISBN: 978-1-63440-081-7 (library hardcover)

1. Counting--Juvenile fiction. 2. Parties--Juvenile fiction. 3. Counting--Fiction. 4. Parties--Fiction. I. Kreloff, Elliot. II. Title.

PZ7.B618652 Cou 2016

[E]   2015938010

Printed in the United States of America
Distributed in the U.S. by Lerner Publisher Services. www.lernerbooks.com

112015   1P   LPSS16

Gigi wants
to have a
birthday party.

But she has
nothing ready
for it.
Zero.

Gigi needs **one** big cake.
Can you find the cake?
Tap it.

Gigi finds **two** large tables.
She adds party plates and party hats.
Trace around each table.

1

2

Gigi picks a party theme.
"Goldilocks and the **Three** Bears"
Does she have enough bears?
Count them.

1

Gigi is putting out **four** different kinds of drinks.
Orange juice, milk, apple juice, and water.

Gigi puts food into **five** big bowls. Her friends will like this food better than porridge.

2

PRETZELS

1

Are all **five** bowls filled?

3

5

4

Gigi collects **six** party games.
Can you tap all the games?

1

2

SLIP-N-SLIDE

3

4

"Pin the Tail on the Bear" is her favorite.

5

6

PIN THE TAIL
ON THE BEAR

Gigi likes balloons.
Help her blow up **seven** balloons, all different colors.

1

2

Puff, puff, puff. **1, 2, 3.**
Puff, puff, puff, puff. **4, 5, 6, 7.**

3

4

5

6

7

It's time to put
the candles on
the cake.

1

Gigi is **eight** years old.
Does she have enough candles?

2 3 4 5 6 7 8

Gigi invites **nine** friends.
Are they all there?
Count them.

1

4

5

6

Gigi buys **ten** gifts.
Nine for her friends.
And **one** for herself.